NANNY'S SPECIAL GIFT

by

Rochelle Potaracke, FSPA

Illustrated by Mark Mitchell

PAULIST PRESS
New York/Mahwah, N.J.

Library of Congress Cataloging-in-Publication Data

Potaracke, Rochelle, 1935–
  Nanny's special gift/by Rochelle Potaracke; illustrated by Mark Mitchell.
    p.   cm.
  Summary: A moment of recognition by his grandmother, who has been forgetting things because of her Alzheimer's disease, reminds seven-year-old Patrick that she is still the Nanny who loves him.
    ISBN 0-8091-6615-1
  [1. Alzheimer's disease—Fiction. 2. Grandmothers—Fiction.] I. Mitchell, Mark, 1951– ill. II. Title.
PZ7.P8397am   1993
[E]—dc 20   93-26093
                                                                                                  CIP
                                                                                                   AC

Published by Paulist Press
997 Macarthur Boulevard
Mahwah, New Jersey 07430

Printed and bound in the
United States of America

Dedicated to
My Mother Nanny

Patrick's feet barely touched the floor as he raced into the kitchen. He skidded to a halt when he saw his Mom setting a basket of plump blackberries on the kitchen table.

When his Mom plopped a fat blackberry into his grubby hand, Patrick smiled. He climbed up on the stool to eat his berry. Then he remembered Nanny who loved the taste of blackberries, and he felt sad.

He pictured Nanny sitting in her big chair in her new home. Why did she have to move away? What made her forget her name? Why was it that every time he thought of her, he had a lump in his throat?

Almost seven, Patrick was small for his age. Red hair capped his head and large brown eyes sparkled from behind silver-rimmed glasses. When he smiled, there were two empty spaces where his baby teeth had been.

St. Benedict Elem. Sch. Lib. 1

He wrapped his sneakers around the rungs of the stool. Patrick's shoulders slumped and his eyes focused on nothing at all as he became lost in thought. He was good at puzzles and solving riddles but he just could not figure out Nanny's problem. She was always forgetting things.

Nanny was his own special grandmother. While planting seeds in early spring, she used to tell stories about mother earth. She made the best carrot cake and fresh bread. When she visited her family, she always had her red leather purse with the four zipper pockets. Baseball cards, pencils, and erasers that looked like animals were in one pocket for Patrick. His little sisters Kerry and Susan would find new barrettes and matching socks. Sometimes Nanny would have applesauce picnics or marshmallow roasts in the back yard. She would use her special tea cups for make-believe coffee.

Now Nanny was in a new home with other old people and had to be helped with everything, even eating. She seldom knew anyone, not even Patrick. This made tears come to his eyes.

"Time for bed." Mom's voice almost scared Patrick. "Tomorrow we will have blackberries and fresh cream for breakfast."

Patrick awoke to good smells coming from the kitchen.

"What's in the oven, Mom?"

"Pies! Blackberry pies!" smiled his mother. "Maybe we can have a blackberry pie picnic today with your friends."

"Yes!" squealed Patrick, wrapping his arms around Mom's waist.

"I'll make a list of people to invite." He got his paper and pencil and sat down at the breakfast table.

"Let's see! Melvin and Carol, Darla and Toots, Aunt Sis, Uncle Dale and Aunt Sandy," said Kerry.

"And we can't forget about Nanny," prompted Patrick.

Everyone was quiet. Patrick looked at his sisters. Then he looked at his Mom and Dad. He loved a picnic with his friends. He loved chasing his cousins and playing games. But what about Nanny? She loved picnics. He looked at the pies cooling on the window sill.

"Mom, may we have a picnic with Nanny's friends?"

Again, everything was quiet. Mom and Dad waited for someone to speak.

"Yes, let's have a picnic with Nanny," said Kerry.

Susan jumped up and down and cried, "A picnic with Nanny! A picnic with Nanny!"

Dad made a phone call and set the picnic time for two o'clock. Mom prepared a gallon of mint tea, and the children chose songs to sing. Patrick could hardly wait to play his drum.

Finally it was picnic time. Over the door of Nanny's new home was a sign, HEART 'N HOME.

Nanny's new home has a name," whispered Patrick. "Gee, it is bigger than I thought. Look at all those people in wheelchairs under the big umbrella. I bet they are older than Nanny."

The children pushed the wheelchairs under the shade tree. Kerry and Susan gently tied bibs on the grannies and passed napkins. Patrick and Dad served the pie as fast as Mom cut it. Everyone watched Nanny's face for a sign of recognition.

Patrick helped Nanny with her pie, and she seemed to enjoy the sweet taste of blackberries. The children sang "Farmer in the Dell," and Patrick marched between wheelchairs. He stepped high and beat the drum in rhythm.

When he came to Nanny's chair he stopped. She looked into his eyes a long time, pulled his chubby face close to hers until their noses were almost touching.

Softly and slowly she said, "I know you!"

Patrick's whole body felt warm and tingly. He put his arms around Nanny's frail body. A big tear rolled down Patrick's nose, and Mom and Dad hugged Patrick and Nanny both. The Nanny look was gone from her eyes, but Patrick still felt good because for a moment Nanny had remembered him. Her smile told him that she loved him and she loved the blackberry pie picnic.

That night Patrick dreamt of Nanny and blackberry pie with ice cream on top, and the gift of Nanny's special smile.